GRADUATION DAY

Adapted by Tracey West

Scholastic Children's Books,
Euston House,
24 Eversholt Street,
London NW1 1DB, UK

A division of Scholastic Ltd
London ~ New York ~ Toronto ~ Sydney ~ Auckland
Mexico City ~ New Delhi ~ Hong Kong

This book was first published in the US in 2016 by Scholastic Inc.
Published in the UK by Scholastic Ltd, 2016

ISBN 978 1407 16274 4

Printed and bound by CPI Group (UK) Ltd, Croydon, CR0 4YY

2 4 6 8 10 9 7 5 3 1

www.scholastic.co.uk

MIX
Paper from
responsible sources
FSC® C020471

CHAPTER 1

"The entire kingdom is buzzing with excitement, Alice!" said joust announcer Herb Herbertson.

"I'm certainly excited, Herb!" agreed his partner, Alice Squires. "And buzzing!"

Herb looked like an ordinary announcer, while Alice was a Squirebot. But they were a lot alike. Both announcers had perfect hair, big smiles, and even bigger voices.

They sat in a booth inside the Joustdome, a gleaming metal and glass dome-shaped arena in the city of Knightonia, the capital of the kingdom of Knighton. Below them, citizens and Squirebots took their seats.

Other Squirebots roamed the aisles, selling snacks and knight souvenirs.

A cheer rose from the crowd as King and Queen Halbert stepped on to their royal balcony. The king's bushy ginger beard could be seen from the farthest seat.

"The king and queen have arrived, so the festivities can officially begin!" Herb announced.

"And they look so radiant for the 151st Annual Knights' Academy Graduation Ceremony!" added Alice.

Herb nodded. "There's a small class of five knights graduating today," he said. "Not much for a knight to do since it's been peaceful here in the realm for more than a hundred years."

"It's going to be an amazing show, featuring Merlok the Magician and Jestro the Royal Jester!" Alice promised. "Now, the big question on everyone's minds – will Princess Macy Halbert be allowed to become a knight of the realm with her classmates?"

"Well, she did graduate second in her class, Alice," Herb reminded her.

Over on the royal balcony, a young woman with dark red hair and freckles was talking to the king and queen. She wore a suit of armour with a red dragon symbol on the chest.

"Dad, you promised I could graduate!" Macy said.

"Princess, you know I don't want you going out and doing any of that messy fighting," King Halbert said.

"I want to be a knight, Dad. It's what I was meant to be." She turned to the queen. "Mum? Talk to him!"

Queen Halbert looked at her husband. "You did promise, dear," she reminded him. "And we haven't had any fighting in our kingdom for a hundred years."

"Oh, all right," King Halbert relented.

"Yes!" Macy cried, rushing off to join the others.

"But no fighting, young lady!" her father called after her.

It was time for the ceremony to begin.

"Let's introduce you to the stars of this show – the newest knights of the realm! Ready for their Graduation Battle-bration!" Herb announced.

Flashing lights shot out of the arena's stage entrance and a rugged knight walked out. He wore silver armour and a dark blue helmet. On his chest was the symbol of a blue-and-white eagle against a dark blue background. He twirled his sword in front of him.

"It's the knights' knight, Clay Moorington!" said Alice. "I don't think anyone expected this country boy to be at the top of his class."

Next emerged a grinning blond knight. His armour bore the symbol of a white horse against a light blue background. He held up a weapon that looked like a long, sharp pole attached to a high-tech handle.

"It's lucky Lance Richmond and his amazingly lithe lance!" declared Alice.

"Wow, I wish I could be him," said Herb.

"Doesn't everyone?" asked Alice.

The third knight flew into the arena on a hoverboard. He had bright red hair, and his armour was accented with green. He held a crossbow and played it like a guitar. His symbol was an orange fox against a green background.

"The thrill-seeker, Aaron Fox!" said Herb.

"He's got 'mad skillz', as the kids say," added Alice.

The fourth knight stomped into the arena. He was twice as big as the others, and he wore a gold helmet with metal horns sticking out of each side. His symbol was a golden bull against a purple background, and he carried a giant, double-bladed axe.

"It's big, bad Axl!" shouted Herb.

"And his big, bad axe!" finished Alice.

After Axl, Macy jumped into the arena, holding a weapon that looked like a big, glowing hammer.

"And the amazing Macy joins in!" cried Herb.

"I never doubted it for a second," said Alice.

"Except when you did just a minute ago," Herb reminded her softly. Then he switched to his big announcer voice. "And we'll be back to start the official Graduation Battle-bration in a few minutes, folks! Stay tuned!"

CHAPTER 2

Backstage at the arena, a crew worked busily to make sure the celebration would go smoothly. In a few minutes, the knights would begin to demonstrate their skills.

Handling the tech were two students at the Knights' Academy, Ava Prentis and Robin Underwood. Ava had brown hair and eyes that always looked as if they were searching for answers. Robin had wavy, sandy blond hair and wore an armour plate over his light blue uniform. His symbol was a cute white chicken on a blue background.

"I wish I could be out there graduating and becoming a knight," grumbled Robin.

"We're only freshmen at the academy, Robin," Ava reminded him. "We're just lucky they let us co-ordinate these dummies."

She pointed to two grinning Squirebots. Each one had a spinning target attached to a short pole on top of his helmet.

"Uh, I meant *target* dummies," Ava corrected herself.

"Hey, we volunteered for this," said the first squire cheerfully.

"Yeah, we like being dummies!" said the second, just as cheerfully.

"Okay, let's give them a good show, everybody!" Robin called out.

"It'll be, um, interesting, I'll guarantee that," said Ava.

Meanwhile, Clay was looking for the other knights. He found Lance reclining on a massage chair in the training room. One Squirebot was trimming his fingernails, and another was polishing his armour.

"Lance, I've prepared a rundown for each

of us on the specific battle moves we should highlight in our Graduation Battle-bration," Clay told him.

He handed Lance a tablet with a digital graphic of the plan. Lance handed it to one of the Squirebots, who tossed it over his shoulder.

"Relax, would you, Super Knight?" Lance asked. "We're going to graduate no matter what."

"It's important that we make a good impression," Clay reminded him.

Lance grinned. "I do that just by being me."

Clay sighed. "Have you seen Merlok? I need to talk to him."

"Who knows what that old wizard is up to," Lance replied. "I'll give you all the advice you need: Just spin your sword around, smile, and they'll all love you. Not as much as they love me, but we all knew that."

Clay rolled his eyes and walked away.

Nearby, Macy, Axl and Aaron were getting ready for the performance.

"You nervous, Axl?" Macy asked.

"Nope," he answered in his deep voice. "I'm hungry."

"You're always hungry," quipped Aaron.

Clay walked in. "But you're about to become an official knight!" he said. "Have you thought about how important that is?"

"Hmmm," Axl mused. "Will it get me an extra slice of cake?"

Music blared through the arena.

"That's our cue," said Aaron, picking up his crossbow and plucking the string as if it was a guitar. "Time for a bow-dacious Battle-bration!"

The crowd clapped and cheered as the Squirebots marched out into the arena. Some of them held wooden targets, while others had targets attached to their helmets. Clay strode into the arena with a determined look on his face.

"The sensational super-swordplay of Clay Moorington!" Herb announced.

Clay spun his sword around in preparation and then charged the first Squirebot.

Swoosh! With one swipe of his blade, he sliced through the digital target on top of the bot's head. The target fizzled out.

Swoosh! Swoosh! Swoosh! Clay jumped from one Squirebot to the next, slicing each target as the crowd hollered its approval.

"Merlok the Magician really helped Clay be the best knight he could be," said Alice.

"Yep, Merlok's friendship and advice paid off," agreed Herb. "Oh look, it's Aaron Fox!"

Aaron zipped into the arena riding his hoverboard. Three Squirebots raced past him, each one balancing a red apple on his helmet.

"Woo-hoo!" cheered Aaron. He aimed his crossbow at the Squirebots and shot an arrow towards them.

Whoosh! The arrow sliced through the first apple, then the second, then the third . . . perfect!

"Aaron Fox, the airborne archer! He's simply out of this world!" said Alice.

Aaron landed next to Clay and fist-bumped him. Then Lance came out, riding his gleaming mecha horse.

"Lance Richmond is always so polished," remarked Herb.

"He's the shiniest knight I've ever seen!" Alice cried, her blue bot eyes gleaming.

Lance lowered his weapon and charged at a Squirebot who was also riding a mecha horse. This was a classic joust. The two would ride at each other head-on, and each had to try to knock off the other using his lance.

The Squirebot charged at Lance with amazing speed. Startled, Lance sped right past him without trying to knock him down.

"Ha ha! You missed!" the bot taunted.

Lance had failed! But that couldn't happen. Not to Lance.

How am I going to fix this? Lance wondered.

CHAPTER 3

Lance turned his head to look at the Squirebot – and his hover horse crashed into the barrier! Acting on instinct, Lance lowered his lance. It bent like a spring, sending him flying across the arena.

Lance tumbled through the air – and then regained his balance. With a cry, he leapt on to the Squirebot's mecha horse, knocking the bot right out of his seat. Lance took control of the horse and flew triumphantly around the arena as the crowd cheered.

"I planned that," he said, as he pulled up to Clay.

"Yeah, sure," Clay replied.

Then big Axl stomped into the arena.

"And here comes Axl! He's always hungry for action," Alice remarked.

"I don't want to get between him and the dinner buffet!" Herb joked.

Axl stared at a giant punch bag full of Squirebots. He was supposed to attack the punching bag with his axe. But that would take too long, and Axl was hungry! Instead, he slammed his axe into the ground.

Boom! The axe's vibrations caused the bag to open and the Squirebots spilled out, crashing into the dirt.

Satisfied, Axl walked over to the others, munching a sandwich.

"Axl the Ever-Hungry gives way to Princess Macy Halbert," announced Herb.

Macy ran out into the arena. Her helmet had metal bars caging in her determined face. She was about to show everyone that she was born to be a knight.

A Squirebot operating a giant mecha-bot

stomped towards her. Macy grunted and charged towards him.

She jumped in the air, landed on the mecha-bot's shoulder, and kicked. As she flew off the robot, it fell forward, right on its face.

The mecha-bot got back on its feet, and Macy activated her power mace. It glowed with power as she leapt forward.

"Ha!" Macy cried, swinging the mace.

Bam! She knocked the mecha-robot's head right off! The crowd cheered as she landed firmly on two feet.

"Wow! That's a-*mace*-ing!" cried Alice, and Herb grimaced at the terrible pun.

Macy joined the other four knights on a platform and it rose up to the royal balcony. The king and queen applauded for them.

"Good citizens of this land!" began King Halbert in a booming voice. "We welcome these new knights of the realm and present them with the symbols of their achievement – the Knightronic Shields of the kingdom, bearing their family crests."

Squirebots came out with four shields bearing symbols that matched the markings on the knights' armour. But there were only four Squirebots and four shields – and none bore the symbol of a dragon.

"Where's my shield, Dad?" Macy asked her father.

"We'll discuss this later," King Halbert said.

Macy gritted her teeth. "This is so unfair."

Axl, Clay, and Lance powered up their shields and turned to the crowd. Aaron jumped on his and hovered above the others.

"Whoa! This makes an awesome hover shield," he said.

Clay frowned. "You know what that is? It's disrespectful. With a capital *D*."

Lance bopped Clay on the head with his lance. "Lighten up, uber-knight. This is supposed to be a party."

King Halbert turned back to the arena.

"Ladies and gentlemen, the Knights' Academy graduates of . . ."

"ROOOOAAAAAR!"

Smoke poured into the arena. Fire exploded from the entrance. A huge monster emerged from the flames, growling and charging the royal booth. His huge body looked as if it was sculpted from molten rock. Lava seemed to flow through his veins. His eyes glowed with yellow fire inside his massive skull, and sharp teeth jutted from his jaw.

Two more glowing monsters emerged behind him!

"Monsters? There haven't been monsters here in a hundred years!" cried Alice.

Herb jumped into her arms. "I'm so scared!"

Queen Halbert grabbed a shield from off the wall and tossed it to her daughter.

"Macy! Use this!" she cried.

The five knights put on their helmets.

"Knights! Defend the people of the realm!"

Clay cried, raising his sword.

The platform lowered and the five knights charged into the arena. Clay swung his sword at the leg of one of the monsters – but as he did so, the monster flickered and disappeared.

"Huh?" wondered Clay, as the monster reappeared, unharmed, in front of him.

Axl swung his battle-axe at a monster, but the big beast dodged the blows. Aaron shot his crossbow at a monster. The arrows glowed brightly when they made contact, but then fizzled out.

Macy jumped up and swung her mace at a monster with all her might. The mace went right through it and she landed on the ground with a thud.

"We've got to co-ordinate our attacks!" Clay yelled. "Lance, drive your monster towards me!"

"Like you know better," Lance scoffed. "I can handle this thing."

He ran towards the nearest monster and threw his lance. It passed right through the monster and hit Axl in the chest. He toppled back, knocking down Macy. Then the lance hit Aaron, knocking him out of the sky. He smashed right into Clay!

The three monsters surrounded the fallen knights. Things looked grim ... until, suddenly, they all vanished!

A tornado of golden light swirled into the arena. The light faded to reveal a wizard in blue robes with a long, white beard.

"Ha! That was a good trick, wasn't it?"

CHAPTER 4

"Tis I, Merlok the Magician!" the wizard announced. He raised his magic staff in the air and sparks shot out of it. "This is supposed to be a celebration!"

Macy turned to Clay and smiled. "It was Merlok. That's a relief."

"Good show, Merlok," said King Halbert. "You truly are the greatest wizard in the realm."

A sad look crossed Merlok's face. "I'm also the only wizard left in the realm."

Then he looked up at the knights and smiled. "Our new knights: While you may be graduating, you must recognize that you still have much to learn. And now, for a little magic."

He swung his staff and pointed it at the knights. Sparkling, golden light poured out.

"*Horus Porus Disappearum!*" the wizard yelled.

The knights vanished into the golden light, and then fireworks exploded over the arena. Merlok bowed to the cheers of the crowd.

Then golden light sparkled again, and the five knights reappeared on the platform. It raised up again as the crowd went wild.

The knights and Merlok went backstage, where Jestro, the court jester, was waiting to perform. He wore a purple-and-blue costume and his face was painted clown white. The bells around his neck jangled as he paced back and forth.

Clay walked up to him. "Hey, Jestro. You're up next," he said. "Don't worry so much. You'll be great."

"I'm kind of nervous, Clay," Jestro admitted. "Never follow a better act, they say, and the people all love Merlok."

"Love is a strong word," Lance chimed in. "I'd say, 'adore', or maybe 'cherish'."

"Look, if anyone laughs at you, I'll give them a haircut with my sword," Clay promised kindly.

"I'm the jester—they're supposed to laugh at me," Jestro said.

"Uh, yeah, that's what I meant," said Clay. "Just stay positive. You'll be fine."

Jestro nodded. "Right. Time for some comedy!"

"That's the spirit!" Clay encouraged, as Jestro walked away.

"Is he going to crash and burn?" Lance whispered.

"No, no. Of course not," Clay said.

"But probably," Lance said.

Clay sighed. "Yeah." He had been Jestro's friend for years. Jestro was a good guy, but a terrible jester.

Jestro knew it, too. But being the court jester was an important job, and he always tried to do his best.

As he stepped out on to the arena floor, he decided to go for a spectacular entrance. He did a handstand and then tried to backflip – and fell right onto his face. The crowd laughed and clapped, thinking it was part of the act.

"You can do this," Jestro told himself, as he picked himself up. "Be funny."

He raised his arms. "Hey, it's good to be here!" he yelled to the crowd. "But I'm always here. I live here!"

Some of the crowd laughed – but the rest groaned. Jestro knew he had to step it up.

He moved on to his spinning plate trick, where he kept six spinning plates balanced on top of six spikes. A good plate spinner could keep it up for a long time – but Jestro's plates crashed after only a few seconds of spinning.

Next, he tried his tablecloth trick. In the centre of the arena was a table topped with a tablecloth and all the ingredients of a royal feast. To impress the crowd, all he had to do was remove the tablecloth without disturbing any of the food.

Jestro yanked the tablecloth – and the food went flying! Apples, carrots, and a pumpkin pie bonked him on the head. Then a roast turkey slipped right over his head! He stumbled around with a turkey on his head, and the crowd booed him.

King Halbert was fond of Jestro and wanted him to do well.

"Do the juggling!" he called out. "Everyone loves juggling!"

Jestro grabbed a sword, a mace and a spear and began to juggle them, humming as he tossed the weapons above his head. Backstage, the knights and Merlok watched the action on a big screen.

"Does he know that's a power mace?" Macy asked.

"Does that make a difference?" Lance wondered.

"It might," Macy replied.

Clay was worried for his friend. "You can do it, Jestro," he said under his breath.

The unimpressed crowd started to boo, so Jestro tried to juggle faster and faster. Sweat broke out on his forehead. He gripped the mace as it came back down, and the weapon powered on.

"*Aaaaaaaaaaah!*" Jestro cried as the charge shocked him. He let go of the mace, and it flew across the arena. The crowd gasped and ducked as the electrically-charged mace flew over their heads.

Then . . . *bam!* It hit the power grid on the arena wall.

The arena lights flickered, then turned off. Soon the power cut spread throughout the city. All of Knightonia was in darkness!

CHAPTER 5

Wow, Alice! Jestro finishes his act with a power cut!" Herb announced, looking around the darkened arena.

"I've heard of bringing the house down, but bringing the power down?" Alice asked, laughing. "Get it?"

"Yeah, I get it," Herb said, shaking his head.

Back on the arena floor, Jestro ran towards the entrance – and banged right into Clay.

"Oh, I'm a horrible failure!" Jestro moaned. "I can't do anything right!"

"Come on, nobody thinks that," Clay assured him.

"You're a horrible failure!" yelled a Squirebot from the stands.

"You can't do anything right!" chimed in another Squirebot.

Jestro burst into tears and ran off.

"Jestro, wait! I want to talk to you!" Clay called after him.

King Halbert knew he had to calm down the frightened crowd. "All is well! Even though darkness falls across the land!"

His words had the opposite effect. The crowd started to panic.

"Uh, I didn't mean it like that," he said. "It is dark, but not evil, world-ending, soul-sucking darkness."

That did it. Everyone began to scream and run.

"You're not helping, dear," said the queen gently.

Jestro had already fled to the dark castle. He walked down the deserted halls, feeling miserable.

"Another big chance, and I blew it!" he scolded himself. "I'm just bad at everything!"

Then a voice came out of nowhere.

"I bet you could be good at being bad, jester!"

Jestro gasped. "Are you talking to me?"

"See any other jesters around?" the voice asked. "No, you're not hearing things. And you're not talking to yourself, either. Come and find me. I'm in Merlok's library."

Curious, Jestro walked to the wizard's library and pushed open the big doors. He cautiously stepped inside.

"This place is usually locked up," he said out loud.

"Yeah, your little power-cut trick unlocked the door," the voice explained.

Jestro walked towards the sound of the voice. It was close. Was it coming from that chair?

He jumped in front of the chair. "Aha!" he cried. But nobody was sitting in it.

"No, no, no," the voice said. "Over here."

Jestro looked around and spotted a large, open book on a stand all by itself. Golden light sparkled around it.

Jestro reached through the light, and it flickered out. He picked up the book and closed it.

"Boo!"

"Aaah!" shrieked Jestro.

There was a face on the cover of the book! Not a picture, but a living face. Two yellow eyes with red pupils glowed above a wide mouth filled with sharp teeth.

"Ha! I love doing that," the book said. "You shoulda seen your face."

"You're a book?" Jestro asked. He still couldn't believe what he was seeing.

"I'm THE book – The Book of Monsters," the book replied. "And I think I could make you the baddest baddie in the realm."

Jestro shook his head. "I don't know . . ."

"You want to have everybody laugh at

you? You want to be a joke?" the book asked. "How many more times do you want to be the laughing stock of the whole kingdom?"

The book's words hit home for Jestro. He thought about all of the people and Squirebots in the stands, laughing at him. His eyes filled with tears again.

"Ah, stop living in the past!" the book said, and then chomped on Jestro's hands.

"Hey, you bit me!" Jestro cried.

"I had to snap you out of sad-face clown-boy mode," said The Book of Monsters. "I can make you somebody! A guy who's respected. I can make you the most feared guy in the whole land. That's gotta be better than spinning plates, right?"

Jestro slowly nodded. "Okay. I'm listening."

"Look around: There's lots of power in these books," the book said. "I know them all. Grab as many as you can and let's break out of this musty old place."

Jestro looked around at the shelves and shelves of books. Did they really hold the power the book said they did? And could he really change his life? Stop being the jester who everyone laughed at?

Maybe. Just maybe.

He started frantically to grab books from the shelf.

"That's it, kid, grab them all," The Book of Monsters instructed. "And you'll need a magic staff to make my pages come to life. Merlok has a dozen of them lying around."

Jestro spotted a staff with a spiked circle on the top. He grabbed it just as Clay walked into the library.

"Jestro? You in here?" Clay called into the dark library. "I wanted to talk to you."

"It's that goody-goody knight!" fumed the book. "Quick, page 205! Wave the magic staff over me and conjure a monster."

"But it's Clay," Jestro said. "He's, like, my friend."

"Nobody's your friend but me, joke-boy! Remember that! Now quick, page 205!"

Jestro quickly leafed through The Book of Monsters. When he found page 205, he saw that it was filled with pictures of monsters. They were all moving, struggling to get out of the book.

Clay spotted him. "Jestro, what are you doing?"

"Do it!" The Book of Monsters hissed.

Jestro pointed the staff at the page. He jumped back as a glowing red arm thrust out of the book. Then another arm. Then a huge, monster body with spiked shoulders, horns, and one enormous eye in its head.

"*Roooooaaaaar!*" bellowed the monster.

"It's Sparkks!" cried The Book of Monsters.

Jestro looked up at the huge creature. Like the monster in Merlok's trick, its body looked as if it was sculpted from molten rock. Lava flowed through its veins. But this was no trick.

This was real.

"What have I done?" Jestro cried.

CHAPTER 6

The Book of Monsters laughed. "This is gonna be one monstrous takedown," he said gleefully. "See, kid? You're good at something. You're good at being bad!"

Sparkks growled, and Clay charged towards him with his sword raised. He jumped in the air and swung the sword down hard towards the monster.

Clunk! It bounced harmlessly off the monster's rock-hard head.

Then Sparkks kicked Clay. The knight flew across the room and slammed into a bookshelf.

Clay tumbled to the floor, picked himself up, and grabbed his sword.

"Rooaaaaar!" Sparkks charged him again.

Clay thought quickly. He looked up and saw the heavy wooden chandelier hanging from the ceiling. He jumped on to a hover disc used to reach the tall library shelves. He rode it until he reached the chandelier. The huge fixture was as big as the monster.

"Aaaargh!" With all his might, Clay swung his sword at the metal pole connecting the chandelier to the ceiling. He jumped to the floor as the heavy, wooden fixture landed right on Sparkks's head.

Sparkks was floored. But he got back up again, growling, and smashed the chandelier into toothpicks.

"More monsters! Make more monsters!" The Book of Monsters cried.

Jestro waved his wand over the book again. From the book sprung Globlins – bouncing fireballs. Then came Bloblins – bigger, bouncing fireballs. Finally came Scurriers – little red creatures with arms and legs that looked as if they were made of pure flame.

Giggling with evil glee, the Globlins and Bloblins bounced at Clay. He batted them aside with his sword. Then came the Scurriers. He swiped at them, too, but there were just too many.

Sensing a moment of weakness, Sparkks swung at Clay with a mighty fist.

Bam! The blow sent the knight flying across the room and crashing to the floor. This time, he couldn't get up.

The library doors swung open, and Merlok stepped inside.

"That crazy ol' Merlok. I hate him!" complained The Book of Monsters. "Now here's our chance – destroy them both!"

The smaller Magma Monsters advanced towards Merlok and the fallen Clay.

"Jestro, stop this!" Merlok cried, pointing his staff at the jester.

He raised the staff over his head and twirled it like a baton. The globe at the end of the staff began to glow with yellow light.

"You ... shall not ... be monstrous!" Merlok cried with great effort, and then slammed the end of the staff on to the floor.

Whoosh! A wave of golden light swept all of the monsters back, even Sparkks. But as soon as the light faded, the monsters charged forward again.

Merlok slowly backed up. Behind him, Clay rose to his feet.

The wizard pointed a hand at Clay. A beam of golden light shot out, zapping him. Clay went flying out of the library doors, and then they slammed shut, locking him out.

"Yes! Finish him!" The Book of Monsters cried.

The monsters ran at Merlok. He began to twirl his staff again, this time over his head.

"Owah! Tagu! Siam!"

His voice got louder with each magic word. When he finished the chant, a tornado of magical golden light swirled around him, growing larger and larger.

Boom! The light exploded, blowing off the roof of the library tower.

The monsters vanished. Jestro and The Book of Monsters went hurtling through the windows and out of the castle. Outside the library door, the vibrations of the explosion knocked Clay out cold.

When he woke up, the other knights were gathered around him.

"Wh-what happened?" Clay asked.

"You tell us, buddy," said Aaron.

Clay got up and forced open the library door. All of the books had been sent flying in the explosion. Stray pages floated in the air like birds.

"Must be the maid's day off," joked Lance.

Then Clay saw it – Merlok's hat, still glowing with scorch marks from the explosion.

The wizard was nowhere in sight.

"Merlok's gone!" Clay cried. "It was Jestro, and he had monsters and a magical book. And he was going to crush us!"

"Jestro? What's wrong with him?" asked Macy.

"He's always been more than a little out there," said Lance.

Clay fell to his knees. "Merlok used some big spell and . . . *boom*. I couldn't save him. I was helpless. I . . . I don't deserve to be a knight."

"Don't blame yourself, Clay," Macy said, trying to console him. "None of us are ready for whatever this is."

"We'd better be," said Clay. "And fast!"

CHAPTER 7

Clay took a deep breath. He knew he had to stay calm. He told the knights everything he could remember about the monsters he had seen. He explained how Merlok had saved him – and sacrificed himself.

He picked up the battered hat. "I still can't believe he's gone," said Clay. "I'm a knight. I should be saving people. Maybe I don't deserve my shield."

Macy put a comforting hand on his shoulder.

In the castle's computer room, Ava was frantically typing on the main console to try to repair the castle's electronic systems.

Robin walked in. "The Squirebots are getting the power back on all over Knighton. It shouldn't take long."

Ava nodded, but she was frowning. "The power failure totally fried the servers. I've got to find a way to get the castle grid up and running."

The digital blue holo screens were up and working, but Ava hadn't been able to get any of the programs to function. Then, without warning, one of the screens began to glow and hum.

"Looks like you did something," Robin said.

"Can't take credit for this," Ava told him.

A mechanical voice came from the screen. "Je-je-je-jes-tro . . ."

"Wait, what was that?" Ava asked. "Jestro?"

At that moment, the jester was walking through the dark forest, carrying The Book of Monsters. They had both survived the blast, but they looked a little battered.

"I can't believe we got blown up," Jestro complained. "I mean, look at me! I'm a wreck. This is awful. How long have we been walking?"

"Ten minutes, bad boy," The Book of Monsters replied.

"That long?" asked Jestro.

"Moan, moan, moan," the book teased. "You're the most delicate evil jester I've ever met. You need to stay focused on your revenge."

"You're getting heavy," Jestro said. "You're a pretty fat book."

He stopped and set the book down on a tree stump.

"I'm not fat, I just have big binding!" the book protested. But he knew that Jestro couldn't go on carrying him for ever. "Okay, open to page three and get out the Book Keeper."

Jestro cautiously opened the book. "I'm

not too sure about this. The last time I tried this I got blasted across the kingdom."

"Oh, don't be such a baby," snapped the book.

Jestro waved the staff over the page and a streak of purple light shot from the book. The light transformed into a small creature. About half as tall as Jestro, the monster was red, with black hair and one yellow eye larger than the other.

Jestro backed away nervously. The little monster walked over to the book, shut it, and hoisted it into his arms. Then he tottered over to Jestro.

"See?" the book said. "Now this little Book Keeper can carry me around. Happy?"

"Fine, but who's going to carry *me*?" Jestro whined.

"Look, you kooky clown! I told you, I'd make you into the best evil force this realm has ever seen, so stop all your complaining or I'm out. Book Keeper, turn me around! I don't want to look at him."

The Book Keeper turned the book around – all the way around, in a complete circle, so that the book was face-to-face with Jestro again.

"No, no! Turn me halfway around! I'm turning my back cover on him!"

The Book Keeper did it right this time.

"All right," said Jestro. "I'll stop moaning. Now tell me again, what's the plan?"

The Book of Monsters outlined his wicked plot.

"It's simple," he said. "We hunt down those evil books that magic Mer-loser blasted all over the kingdom. The more evil books we get, the more evil we'll be."

"You mean the more evil *I'll* be, right?" asked Jestro.

"Yeah, yeah, right. Now let's go." He sniffed the air. "I smell nasty."

"Actually, you do have a pretty musty odour," Jestro said.

The book got defensive. "I've been on a shelf for a hundred years! Without any deodorant!"

Then the three of them headed further into the dark, spooky forest.

CHAPTER 8

Inside the Joustdome, Squirebots worked to try to restore power. Others were cleaning up after the Graduation Battlebration.

Macy walked into the training room and found Clay angrily hacking a wooden target to pieces with his sword.

"Clay, we need a plan. We need to be ready for anything," she told him.

"I know," Clay said, not taking his eyes off his next target. "I think better when I'm training."

He threw a broken piece of target in the air and jumped up to reach it.

Whack! He sliced it right in two.

Nearby, Lance was face down on a massage table as a Squirebot karate-chopped his back.

"A little to the left, Dennis," Lance instructed.

Clay glared at Lance. With a cry, he angrily hurled his sword at a target just above Dennis's head. The sword hit the bull's-eye, and the Squirebot ran away, screaming.

Lance looked up. "Hey! You ruined my midday massage."

Clay marched up to Lance. "Most of the city's without power! Merlok is gone! Dark magic may be loose! You realize we're dealing with epic, life-altering events here?"

"Of course. You know how tense I am right now?" Lance asked, sitting up. "I have a knot in my shoulder the size of a grapefruit."

"I don't have time to massage your ego. We need to train!" Clay said.

In one swift motion, he pulled the sword out of the target and sliced through the legs of the massage table. Lance jumped off as the broken table clattered to the floor.

Angry now, Lance pressed a button on the handle of his lance. The pole slid out and he charged towards Clay.

Clang! Metal clashed against metal as the lance and the sword hit each other.

"Who put you in charge?" Lance asked. "You're not the boss of me."

Clang! Clang! Clang!

"I'm the only one here who truly lives by the Knights' Code!" Clay replied, as the two traded blows.

Clang! Clang!

"Boys! This is totally unproductive," Macy said, but Lance and Clay ignored her and kept battling.

"Axl! A little help here!" Macy called out.

Axl gulped down the last bite of the chicken leg he was eating and came over. He picked up Clay in one hand and Lance in the other.

"Come on, guys, you're giving me an upset stomach," Axl said.

Clang! The two knights kept fighting, even though their feet were dangling above the floor.

"I see you had to call in reinforcements. Not something a *true* leader would do," Lance told Clay.

"At least I'm not lying around rubbing people up the wrong way!" Clay shot back.

Macy sighed, shook her head, and left the training room. Those two were hopeless!

Over in the castle, Robin and Ava were busy at work in the computer room. Robin had just attached radar dish helmets to five Squirebots.

"Radar helmets are working," he said. "Now what?"

Ava called up an image of Knightonia on her screen. "Put these guys in strategic locations around the city and we can triangulate the origin of that weird signal we got earlier," she replied.

"Ready!" the Squirebots said excitedly. They turned on their radar helmets, then headed out to locate the signal.

CHAPTER 9

The Book of Monsters sniffed the air as the Book Keeper moved him through the dark forest. Jestro followed behind them. He kept waving his staff in the air and making weird faces.

"What are you doing? Other than being annoying?" the book asked him.

"I'm practising my evil poses," Jestro replied. "You said practice makes perfect."

"I meant practise being *actually* bad, not a poser," said the book. "You need to be ready to use me to call forth nasty, awful monsters."

"Okay," said Jestro. Then he moved away and turned back again, snarling and waving his arms in the air. "How about this one? Haaaa!"

The Book of Monsters rolled his eyes. "Oh, I am terrified," he said in a voice that proved he clearly wasn't. "You make me want to cry for my mummy, Jestro the Evil."

Jestro nodded. "Jestro the Evil? I like the sound of that!"

The book sniffed the air again. "Hey, I smell something! It's that way."

The Book Keeper ran off with The Book of Monsters.

"No, the *other* way!" cried the book.

The Book Keeper changed direction.

"Oh yeah!" said the book, sniffing again. "I smell a magic book nearby. And it smells *bad*."

Jestro looked around nervously as they walked deeper into the forest. Even though it was morning, no sunlight came through the trees here. No birds sang. He shivered.

Then a white rabbit hopped towards him.

Jestro was relieved to see something so cute in this gloomy place.

"Look, it's a harmless little bunny!" he said, reaching towards it.

The bunny's eyes turned red, and it growled, revealing sharp fangs. Jestro backed away in fear. "*Ahh!* That's the most vicious rodent I've ever set eyes on!" he yelled.

"I know why," said The Book of Monsters. "Look! The Book of Evil!"

There, lodged in the dirt, was a book with a purple cover adorned with a glowing yellow symbol.

"It doesn't look so bad," Jestro said.

He picked it up—and black ooze crawled out of it on to his hands, and then spread over his body. His costume changed from purple and blue to dark blue and red. A strange yellow glow came over his eyes. The points on his jester hat curled up to look like horns.

"Quick! Quick! Feed me!" cried The Book of Monsters.

Jestro tossed The Book of Evil to The Book of Monsters. He caught it in his mouth and greedily chewed and swallowed it down.

"Let's party!" yelled The Book of Monsters with an evil cackle.

Back in the castle, Ava studied the map of the city. The Squirebots with radar helmets showed up as blinking dots.

Robin's face popped up on the screen. "That's the last radar Squirebot. How's it look?" he asked her.

"Great," she replied. "Grid is set, five-by-five."

Macy walked in. "Radar Squirebots? What are you guys doing?"

"Trying to restore the castle's operating systems and power," Ava answered. "But we've been getting weird messages."

"Messages?" Macy asked.

Suddenly, Ava's computer screen flickered. Lights flashed. A blurry shape appeared on the screen.

Then a voice crackled from the screen. "Jes . . . Att . . . Castle . . . Jes . . . tro."

"There it is!" Ava cried. Then she frowned. "I can't locate it."

"Who is it?" Macy asked. "What do they want?"

The screen flickered, and then it went dark.

"It's gone," Ava said. "But I may have got a fix on it from the Wi-Fi source."

Macy looked worried. "What's going on?" she wondered.

Early the next morning, the knights returned to the training room in the Joustdome. Aaron zipped around the room on his hover shield, doing flips and other tricks. He hovered in the air next to Axl, whose shield was piled high with food.

"This Knightronic Shield is the best hoverboard I've ever had," Aaron reported.

"Mine works best as a plate," said Axl. He brought the shield to his open mouth, tipped the food inside, and swallowed it in one gulp. Then he let out a loud burp.

Nearby, Clay and Lance were *still* trading blows with their weapons.

"Respect the Knights' Code," said Clay, as his sword clanked weakly against Lance's shield.

"Respect my nap time," said Lance, stifling a yawn.

He swept at Clay with his lance, and the two knights fell on top of each other, exhausted.

"You take nothing seriously," said Clay.

"And you're super bossy," Lance countered.

Macy entered and looked around the room. Aaron was doing tricks on his hover shield, Axl was eating, and Clay and Lance looked as if they had been fighting each other all night. She shook her head.

How were they supposed to battle monsters if they couldn't work together and come up with a plan?

CHAPTER 10

Let's make some monsters!" Jestro cried.

"Some evil, nasty monsters!" agreed The Book of Monsters. He could feel the power from The Book of Evil flowing through him.

Jestro threw open the book. On every page, monsters moved and called to them, anxious to get out.

Jestro waved his wand over the open pages. "Nasty, evil monsters, come forth and serve me! Make the folks around us wet their pants and flee!"

Globlins, Bloblins, and Scurriers bounced out of the book, cackling and laughing.

"How great is this?" Jestro asked. "More!"

He waved his staff again, and two huge monsters appeared. One was Sparkks, the one-eyed giant who had been released in the library. The second was just as tall as Sparkks, with a body glowing fiery red, a mouth full of nasty teeth, two glowing yellow eyes, and a grey, curved horn on each side of his head.

"Burnzie and Sparkks, ready to serve you," the two monsters said.

"Excellent!" said Jestro. "I'll have a tuna sandwich with pickle and coleslaw."

"To serve your plan for evil vengeance, joke-boy!" The Book of Monsters snarled. "They're horrible monsters, not waiters."

"Right," said Jestro. "Then let's go hassle those jerks in the castle!"

In the castle, the knights didn't know that a monster army was on its way to attack them. Clay was working out doing a bench press, lifting a metal pole with a Squirebot hanging on each end.

"I agree with you, Macy," Clay was saying. "We should be training and ready for everything."

Lance and Axl were playing a video game.

"You guys worry too much," said Lance.

Macy shook her head. "We need to get organized and get out there and be knights."

"Woo-hoo!"

Aaron whizzed by on his hover shield and grabbed Macy by the arm, taking her with him.

"You've tried all day to get everyone organized, Macy," he said, as they flew around the training room. "Maybe you should just let them . . . chill."

"Chill? Just chill, Aaron?" Macy asked angrily. She hopped on to the hover shield and turned to face him. "The kingdom needs us. My father needs us. Whoa!"

They crashed into a stack of boxes. Macy tumbled off the board and tossed a box that had landed on her head. She sighed. "And I want to prove to him so badly that I can be a knight."

Aaron sat down next to her. "I get it. You'll get your chance."

"Yeah, but when?" Macy asked.

Whaa! Whaa! Whaa! An alarm rang through the Joustdome, and a red light flashed.

"Uh, sooner than you think?" Aaron asked.

As the knights raced to gear up for battle, Jestro and The Book of Monsters approached the castle with their army of monsters.

"I feel ... a little queasy," Jestro said. Even though he was trying to be evil, the idea of attacking the castle didn't feel right to him.

"Don't puke on me," snapped the book. "Just remember: This is your chance to get back at all those people who laughed at you. Who think you're nothing but a joke."

Jestro closed his eyes and remembered everyone laughing and pointing at him. He opened them again, and his eyes were blazing.

"It's time to attack!" he yelled.

The Book of Monsters grinned. "He's *baaaack*, and he's *baaaad*!" he cheered. "Time to take down that castle!"

"Burnzie and Sparkks, fling 'em!" ordered Jestro.

The two big monsters scooped up Globlins and hurled them at the castle. They flew over the walls of the castle and landed on the royal balcony.

Two Squirebots leapt in front of the king and queen, their swords raised.

"Protect the king!" yelled one.

"Protect the queen!" yelled the other.

Bop! Bop! Bop! The Globlins knocked them both down.

"It's an invasion!" the king cried.

The castle gates opened and a squad

of Squirebots ran out to try to stop the Globlin onslaught. They trembled when they saw Burnzie and Sparkks, but they bravely faced them.

"Hold your ground!" ordered their leader.

Whomp! Burnzie reached down and tossed them aside, leaving only the leader. The Squirebot raised his sword.

"Have at you!" he cried.

Burnzie breathed on the sword, and it glowed with red-hot heat. The Squirebot dropped it and ran away, screaming.

Laughing, Burnzie picked up a Globlin and rolled it towards an advancing squad of Squirebots. The Globlin slammed into the first one, and the rest of them toppled over like bowling pins.

Sparkks laughed. "Yes!" he cried, high-fiving Burnzie.

Then the castle gates opened again. This time, it revealed the five knights, ready for battle! Their shields and weapons were glowing with power.

"Time to show everyone that we deserved to graduate from the Knights' Academy!" said Clay.

CHAPTER 11

Okay knights, let's hit them on the right flank," Clay said.

The five knights charged forward.

Clay jumped up and kicked Sparkks in the head. Then he landed on the opposite side of the monster. Sparkks turned around and aimed a punch at Clay. Clay dodged it, and the monster's fist hit the road and broke the concrete.

Clay jumped up to attack Sparkks again, but this time the monster's fist hit its mark. Clay fell backwards with a thud.

Lance stood over him, grinning.

"You deal with monsters your way, I'll deal with monsters my way," he said.

He charged at Burnzie with his lance extended. Burnzie grabbed the weapon and lifted Lance off the ground.

"Puny knight," he taunted, and then tossed Lance aside. He landed next to Clay and gave him a sheepish grin.

Aaron flew around the courtyard on his hover shield.

"Here comes the stick!" he cried, shooting at Globlins with his crossbow. Blue energy arrows shot out and hit their targets – but the arrows just bounced off the Globlins!

Macy wasn't having any luck, either. She pounded at the Globlins with her mace, but they kept popping right back.

"I hate these hot little things!" she complained.

Axl swatted at the Globlins with his battle-axe.

"Get off me!" he growled, as a swarm of them piled on him.

Jestro and The Book of Monsters advanced towards the battle zone.

"The knights," said Jestro anxiously.

"They're nothing!" said The Book of Monsters. "You wiped the floor with that Moorington guy."

"But Clay was always good to me," Jestro said.

"Don't go soft on me!" the book snapped. "He still let people laugh and laugh. They *all* laughed at you."

Up on the royal balcony, a Globlin came flying towards King Halbert. Queen Halbert jumped up and kicked it away.

"Lay off my king!" she said angrily.

More Globlins flew toward the balcony, and the queen grabbed the nearest weapon she could find – a Squirebot. She picked him up and used him as a baseball bat to knock away the little red monsters.

Down below, the knights did their best to protect the castle gates, but the monsters kept coming.

"Hold them off! Hold them off!" Clay yelled.

Lance batted away Globlins with his lance, but they kept bouncing back.

"Crazy burning blobs!" he yelled. "These weapons have almost no effect on these monsters."

"And you've got the best weapons money can buy," Macy remarked, as she smacked two Globlins with her mace.

"I know, right?" Lance replied.

"We've got to get organized," Macy said. "We're being overrun!"

Clay jumped and landed next to her. "Just keep fighting!" he said, hitting two Globlins with his sword.

The Globlins just kept coming and coming. They swarmed over Axl until he couldn't fight them off any more. They knocked him down and bounced on his armour.

"I've decided I don't like monsters," he announced.

Aaron zipped up on his hover shield. "They don't like you either, big guy!" he said. He shot at the Globlins with his energy arrows.

The Book of Monsters grinned at Jestro. "I told you they'd be no match for you and your monsters."

Jestro laughed with glee. "I'm good at something!" he cried happily. Then his smile turned into an evil snarl. "I'm good at being bad!"

In another part of the castle, Ava and Robin followed a radar Squirebot into Merlok's library.

"I finally locked on to it," Ava said. "This is the source of that mysterious signal."

"Here?" asked Robin. "This place has been blasted to bits."

Ava walked over to the computer console and turned it on. A blue holographic screen appeared in front of her. She quickly typed on the keyboard. The blue screen suddenly turned golden yellow.

"Whoa, power surge," said Robin.

"What's going on?" Ava wondered.

Golden light poured from the screen. It filled the library. Then the light took shape on top of Merlok's desk.

"I am Merlok!" the golden figure cried.

Ava and Robin gasped. The figure of Merlok had appeared on the holographic projector.

"No way! Merlok!" Robin cried. "Well, more like Merlok 2.0."

"Merlok 2.0?" Ava asked. "Really? That sounds like an operating system from twenty years ago." She thought for a moment. "I guess it's better than Merlok Beta, but not by much."

"You're missing the point," Merlok 2.0 said. "I'm here to help you."

"Yeah, now he's like a digital wizard," Robin said. "This is pretty awesome."

"We'll work on the naming thing after we fight some monsters," said Ava.

"Yes!" cheered Merlok 2.0. "Get ready for NEXO Scan!"

Ava quickly patched into Clay's communication system. Clay heard her voice through his shield.

"Clay, it's Ava," she said.

"I'm a little busy right now, Ava," Clay said, as he struck Sparkks with a blow from his sword.

"I need you to stop fighting and point your shield at the sky," she said.

"What?" Clay asked.

"Just do it!" Ava said firmly.

Clay did it. He pointed his shield at the sky.

Energy crackled in the air above him, and a holographic golden dragon took shape! The dragon exploded into golden energy that downloaded into Clay's shield, charging it.

"NEXO Power: Dragon of Justice!" Merlok 2.0 yelled.

CHAPTER 12

The power surged through Clay's shield into his sword and armour. Glowing with golden power, he swung at a Globlin. The creature dissolved into a puff of black smoke and then vanished.

"It's Merlok!" Clay realized. He called out to the other knights. "Raise your shields up. Do it!"

Lance, Macy, Aaron and Axl obeyed. The NEXO Power downloaded into their shields and powered up their weapons and armour, too.

Merlok's voice came through their shields. "Show them the power of the NEXO KNIGHTS heroes!"

Lance's lance sliced through the fiery Globlins.

Poof! They turned into smoke and disappeared.

Macy smashed them with her mace.

Poof! Globlins gone.

Poof! Poof! Poof! Aaron took out the Globlins with his arrows.

Bam! Axl sent them packing with his battle-axe.

Jestro looked on in horror.

"What's going on? How are they destroying my monsters?" he asked.

"I ain't The Book of Answers, but I bet that Merlok has something to do with this," guessed The Book of Monsters.

With the Globlins under control, Lance and Clay charged the big monsters.

"Puny monster!" Lance cried, striking Burnzie with his lance.

Sparkks cried out as Clay struck him with his sword.

Both monsters transformed into purple smoke. They flew back into the pages of The Book of Monsters.

"I completely approve of the new Merlok!" said Clay happily.

"Now what?" asked Jestro.

"A new lesson," said The Book of Monsters. "He who fights and runs away, lives to fight another day. Retreat!"

The Book Keeper started to run – right towards the knights!

"No! Retreat the *other* way! The other way, dopey monster!" the book yelled.

The Book Keeper turned and ran away from the castle. Jestro followed. The knights raised their weapons triumphantly.

The battle over, they went to the library to join Robin, Ava, and Merlok 2.0.

Clay looked in wonder at the holographic image of the wizard.

"It's nice to have you back, Merlok," he said.

"I am now Merlok 2.0," corrected the wizard.

"He's a three-dimensional holographic projection now," explained Ava. "He was absorbed into the computer system by his magical blast."

Merlok 2.0 looked at Clay. "Clay, you must prepare," he said. "Jestro will be back and you will face a dire threat from his monsters."

"Where do those creatures come from?" Clay asked.

"That's, well, a long story," Merlok replied.

The king and queen entered the library.

"Merlok, my old friend, it is nice to know that you are still with us," the king said.

"In whatever form you're in," added the queen.

Axl and Aaron picked up two controllers.

"Check this out. He's got a built-in game centre," said Aaron.

Little video-game knights started

marching around Merlok 2.0.

"What's going on?" Merlok 2.0 asked.

"I'm about to get the new high score," said Axl.

"Guys! Guys! You're overloading the circuits!" Ava warned.

"Ahh!" Merlok 2.0 cried. "My digital magic only provides power for—"

The library went dark. The power had gone out once again!

"Darkness has fallen across the land," King Halbert announced.

Macy sighed. "Dad, please. Can somebody find a torch?"

Clay laughed. It felt good to have saved the castle from an army of monsters. With the help of Merlok 2.0 and his fellow knights, Clay knew they would be able to defeat any evil that threatened Knighton. Now, if they could just find a light switch . . .